Alameda County
# LIBRARY
*...Infinite possibilities*

NHUSD/EVENSTART PROGRAM

# POOH GOES
# VISITING

A. A. MILNE

# Pooh Goes Visiting

Adapted by Stephen Krensky

With decorations by
ERNEST H. SHEPARD

Dutton Children's Books
New York

This presentation copyright © 2002 by the Trustees of the Pooh Properties
From *Winnie-the-Pooh,* copyright © 1926 by E.P. Dutton & Co., Inc.;
copyright renewal 1954 by A. A. Milne.

CIP Data is available.

Published in the United States 2002 by Dutton Children's Books,
a division of Penguin Putnam Books for Young Readers
345 Hudson Street, New York, New York 10014
www.penguinputnam.com

Printed in China
First Edition
ISBN 0-525-46821-8
1 3 5 7 9 10 8 6 4 2

# CONTENTS

# 1

## POOH STEPS OUT

Winnie-the-Pooh was walking

through the forest one day,

humming proudly to himself.

He had made up a little hum

that <u>very</u> morning,

as he was doing his Stoutness Exercises.

"*Tra-la-la, tra-la-la,*" he said,

stretching up as high as he could go.

And then "*Tra-la-la, tra-la—oh, help!—la,*"

as he tried to reach his toes.

He had said the hum over and over

until he had learned it by heart.

Now he was humming it

right through, properly.

Well, he was humming this hum,

when suddenly he came to a sandy bank.

And in the bank was a large hole.

"Aha!" said Pooh.

"If I know anything about anything,

that hole means Rabbit.

And Rabbit means Company.

And Company means Food."

*Tra-la-la, tra-la-la,*

*Tra-la-la, tra-la-la,*

*Rum-tum-tiddle-um-tum.*

*Tiddle-iddle, tiddle-iddle,*

*Tiddle-iddle, tiddle-iddle,*

*Rum-tum-tum-tiddle-um.*

So he put his head back into the hole.

"Hallo, Rabbit, isn't that you?" he said.

"No," said Rabbit in a different sort of voice.

"But isn't that Rabbit's voice?" Pooh asked.

"I don't *think* so," said Rabbit.

"It isn't *meant* to be."

"Oh!" said Pooh.

He took his head out of the hole

and had another think.

Then he put it back in.

"Well," he said,

"could you very kindly

tell me where Rabbit is?"

"He has gone to see his friend

Pooh Bear," said Rabbit.

"But this *is* Me!" said Bear,

very much surprised.

"What sort of Me?" asked Rabbit.

"Pooh Bear."

"Are you sure?" said Rabbit.

"Quite, quite sure," said Pooh.

"Oh, well, then," said Rabbit,

"come in."

# 2

## POOH HAS A LITTLE SOMETHING

So Pooh pushed and pushed and

pushed his way through the hole,

and at last he got in.

"You were quite right," said Rabbit,

looking at him all over.

"It *is* you."

"Who did you think it was?" said Pooh.

"Well, I wasn't sure," said Rabbit.

"You know how it is in the forest.

One has to be *careful*.

What about a mouthful of something?"

Pooh always liked a little something

at eleven o'clock in the morning,

and he was very glad to see Rabbit

getting out the plates and mugs.

"Well, good-bye," said Rabbit.

"If you're sure you won't have

any more."

"*Is* there any more?" asked Pooh quickly.

Rabbit took the covers off the dishes.

"No, there isn't," he said.

"I thought not," said Pooh,

nodding to himself.

"Well, good-bye, then."

So Pooh started to climb

out of the hole.

He pulled with his front paws

and pushed with his back paws.

In a little while his nose

was out in the open again…

and then his ears…

and then his front paws…

and then his shoulders…

and then—

"Oh, help!" said Pooh.

"I'd better go back.

Oh, bother!" said Pooh.

"I shall have to go on.

I can't do either!" said Pooh.

"Oh, help *and* bother!"

# 3

# POOH REMAINS IN A TIGHT PLACE

Now by this time

Rabbit wanted to go for a walk too.

Finding his front door full,

he went out the back,

and came round to Pooh.

"Hallo, are you stuck?"

he asked.

"N-no," said Pooh carelessly.

"Just resting and thinking

and humming to myself."

"Here, give us a paw," said Rabbit.

Pooh stretched out a paw,

and Rabbit pulled and

pulled and pulled....

*"Ow!"* cried Pooh. "You're hurting."

"The fact is," said Rabbit,

"you're stuck."

"It all comes," said Pooh crossly,

"of not having front doors

big enough."

"It all comes," said Rabbit sternly,

"of eating too much.

I thought at the time—

only I didn't want

to say anything—

that one of us was eating

too much.

And I knew it wasn't *me*.

Well, well, I shall go and fetch

Christopher Robin."

Christopher Robin lived at the other

end of the forest.

When he came back with Rabbit,

he saw the front half of Pooh.

"Silly old Bear," he said,

in such a loving voice

that everybody felt

quite hopeful again.

"I was just beginning to think," *take*

said Pooh, sniffing slightly,

"that Rabbit might never be able

to use his front door again.

And I should *hate* that."

"So should I," said Rabbit.

"Use his front door again?"

said Christopher Robin.

"Of course he'll use

his front door again."

"Good," said Rabbit.

"If we can't pull you out, Pooh,"

said Christopher Robin,

"we might push you back."

Rabbit scratched

his whiskers thoughtfully.

He pointed out that,

once Pooh was pushed back,

he was back.

Of course, nobody was more glad

to see Pooh than *he* was.

Still, some lived in trees

and some lived underground, and—

"You mean I'd *never* get out?" said Pooh.

"I mean," said Rabbit,

"that having got *so* far,

it seems a pity to waste it."

Christopher Robin nodded.

"Then there's only one thing to be done,"

he said. "We shall have to wait

for you to get thin again."

"How long does getting thin take?"

asked Pooh anxiously.

"About a week, I should think,"

said Christopher Robin.

"But I can't stay here for a *week!*"

said Pooh.

"You can *stay* here all right,

silly old Bear,"

said Christopher Robin.

"It's getting you out which is

so difficult."

"We'll read to you," said Rabbit cheerfully.

"And I hope it won't snow.

And I say, as you're taking up

a good deal of room,

*do* you mind if I use your back legs as

a towel-horse?

"Because, I mean, there they are—

doing nothing—

and it would be very convenient."

"A week!" said Pooh gloomily.

*"What about meals?"*

"I'm afraid no meals,"

said Christopher Robin,

"because of getting thinner quicker."

Pooh began to sigh,

and then found he couldn't

because he was so tightly stuck.

A tear rolled down his eye.

"Then," he said,

"would you read a Sustaining Book

that would help and comfort

a Wedged Bear in Great Tightness?"

"Of course," said Christopher Robin.

# 4

## POOH REGAINS
## HIS FREEDOM

So for a week

Christopher Robin read

at the North end of Pooh.

And Rabbit hung his washing

on the South end.

And in between Pooh felt himself

getting slenderer and slenderer.

At the end of the week

Christopher Robin said, *"Now!"*

He took hold of Pooh's front paws,

and Rabbit took hold

of Christopher Robin.

And all of Rabbit's friends and

relations took hold of Rabbit.

Then they all pulled together....

For a long time Pooh only said

*"Ow!"*... and *"Oh!"*...

Then, all of a sudden, he said *"Pop!"*

just as if a cork

were coming out of a bottle.

And Christopher Robin and Rabbit

and all Rabbit's friends and relations

went head-over-heels backwards . . .

and on the top of them

came Winnie-the-Pooh—free!

So, with a nod of thanks to his friends,

Pooh went on with his walk

through the forest,

humming proudly to himself.

But Christopher Robin

looked after him lovingly,

and said to himself,

"Silly old Bear!"